TOBIAS
AND HIS BIG RED
SATCHEL

Written and Illustrated by

SUNNY B. WARNER

Alfred A. Knopf : New York

Text set in *Melior Italic*. Composed at *Philmac Typographers, New York*.
Printed at *Reehl Litho Co., New York*. Bound at *H. Wolf, New York*.
Typography by *Tere LoPrete*

L.C. Catalog card number 61-6046

This is a Borzoi Book, published by Alfred A. Knopf, Inc.

For my son GEOFFREY, with love

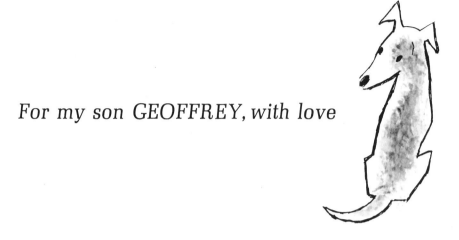

"My heavens, Tobias," his mother said,
"That satchel you carry is heavy as lead!
It's always beside you, both indoors and out,
Why is it you carry that satchel about?"

Tobias replied, "Well now that you ask,
Carting this satchel is rather a task,
But I carry it since I might need any minute
The terribly usable things that are in it.

Just wait till I tell you the fabulous fix
I found an old man in at quarter of six.
His whiskers all pigtailed hung down to his toes
(Unless they were braided they tickled his nose).

His wonderful whiskers hung down to his feet
But while he was pouring cement for a street,
They caught in the walk as it started to set...
And but for my scissors, he'd be there yet!"

Said his mother, "Tobias, I'm proud as can be
That you used your scissors to set him free
But couldn't you possibly do without
This heavy old saw that you carry about?"

"Just wait till I tell you what happened to me
On Saturday morning at quarter to three
I came on a sight never seen before—
A house that hadn't a single door!

And I heard the carpenter say with a shout,
'I'VE BUILT MYSELF IN AND I CAN'T GET OUT!'

I pulled out that saw, and quick as I could,
I sawed him a door right out of the wood!"

"My goodness, Tobias, I certainly see
How useful a saw in that satchel can be—
But couldn't you lighten it over a pound
If you left out this rope that you carry around?"

"Well here is what happened to me on the fourth,
While strolling around by the Pole way up North—
I spied some explorers afloat on the sea
On an iceberg the shape of a bended up knee.

Their toes were all frozen, their noses were pink,
They were freezing and sneezing and starting to sink!
I got out that rope, and I hauled them all in,

And they gave me this medal, stuck on with a pin."

Said his mother, "Tobias, I'm proud as can be
That you had your rope and could set them free
But couldn't you possibly do without
This heavy old shovel you carry about?"

"Just picture the sight that confronted my eye
While swimming the ocean one day in July—
Way up on a sand bar, all stranded and stuck,
Was a baby whale, big as a trailer truck!

His family was worried, but what could they do?
They were swimming around in a terrible stew.
Well, I pulled out that shovel, and quick as could be,
I dug out a channel from him to the sea!"

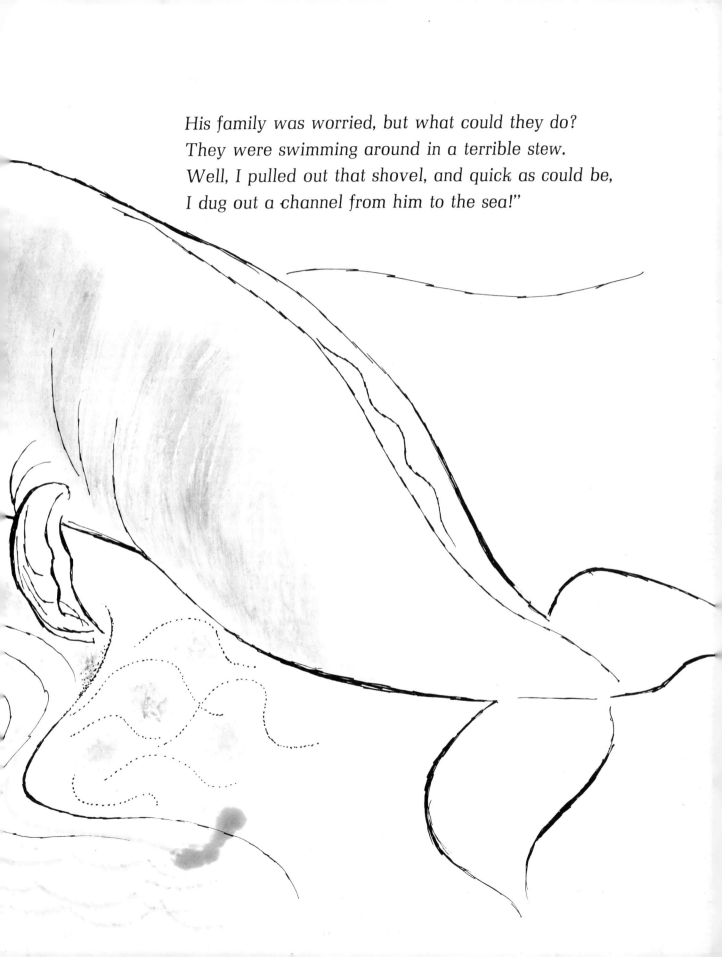

"My goodness, Tobias, I certainly see
That you needed a shovel to set him free—
But couldn't you lighten that satchel a bit
By taking this hammer and nails out of it?"

"Well here's what I found all drenched in the rain
As I was exploring the forests of Spain—

A bird who was hatching her eggs in a tree
As wet and bedraggled as she could be.

I went right to work,
      got some wood from the trees,
And nailed up a house for her,
      neat as you please!"

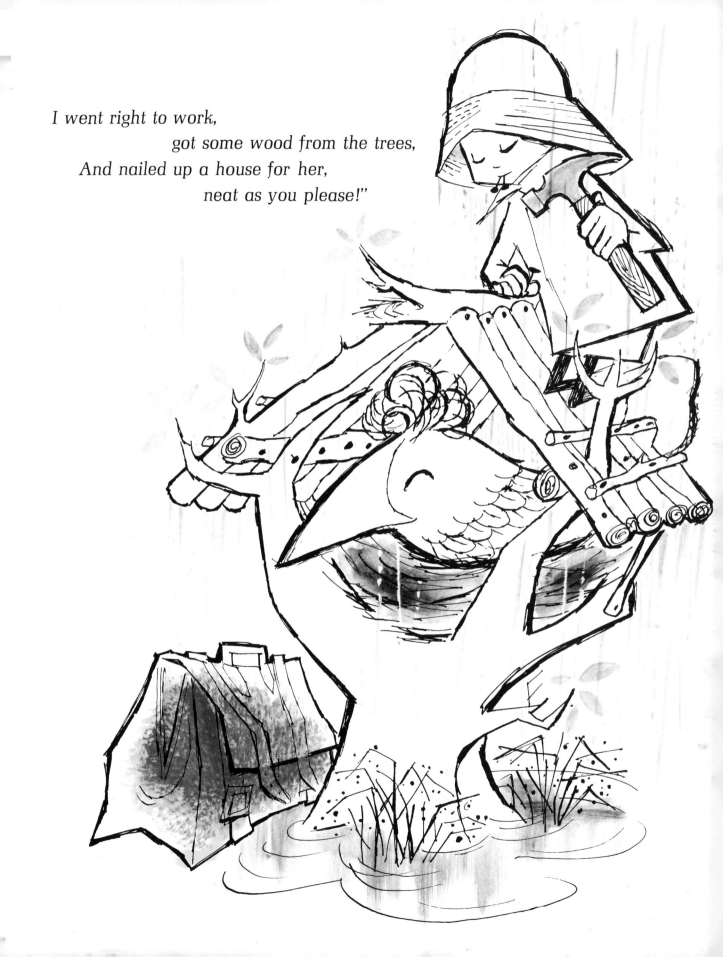

"My goodness, Tobias, I certainly see
How handy a hammer and nails can be—
But couldn't you possibly do without
This big iron bar that you carry about?"

"In the woods I discovered a tortoise last night
Who was turned on his back and just couldn't get right.
He'd fallen asleep on what seemed to be clover,
But it grew so fast that it turned him over!
Then what a surprise when he woke up and found
The sky underneath him instead of the ground!

I worked with that crowbar till over he fell,

And he carried me home on the top of his shell."

Said his mother, "Tobias, it's plain as can be
You needed that crowbar to set him free—

But that satchel's so <u>heavy</u> for someone your size,"
His poor mother pleaded, with tears in her eyes.
"Though you need all the rest, you could surely leave out
These great heavy bolts that you carry about."

"It's true," said Tobias, "I've not used them yet.
We'll leave them out, mother,

and please don't you fret—

It's heavy all right,
          but I'm strong for my size,"
And he reached for his satchel,
          but what a surprise!

In his hand was the handle, but there on the floor
Sat the satchel exactly the same as before.

"Those BOLTS are what's needed,"
    he said to his mother,
"I thought they'd be handy
    in some way or other."

He went right to work, and when he was through,
His big red satchel was as good as new.

"It just goes to show that I can't do without
Any one of the things that I carry about.
YOU understand, mother," Tobias said,
And he picked up his satchel, and went up to bed.